A Whiff of Pine, a Hint of Skunk

DISCARD

A Whiff of Pine,

Deborah Ruddell   Illustrated by Joan Rankin

Margaret K. McElderry Books • New York   London   Toronto   Sydney

A forest of poems

a Hint of Skunk

Margaret K. McElderry Books

An imprint of Simon & Schuster Children's Publishing Division

1230 Avenue of the Americas, New York, New York 10020

Text copyright © 2009 by Deborah Ruddell

Illustrations copyright © 2009 by Joan Rankin

Book design by Krista Vossen

The text for this book is set in Filosofia.

The illustrations for this book are rendered in watercolor.

Manufactured in China

10 9 8 7 6 5 4 3 2

Library of Congress Cataloging-in-Publication Data

Ruddell, Deborah.

A whiff of pine, a hint of skunk /

Deborah Ruddell ; illustrated by Joan Rankin.—1st ed.

p. cm.

ISBN-13: 978-1-4169-4211-5 (hardcover)

ISBN-10: 1-4169-4211-4 (hardcover)

1. Nature—Juvenile poetry. 2. Children's poetry, American.

I. Rankin, Joan, ill. II. Title.

PS3618.U337W54 2009

811'.6—dc22

2007038023

For Brian, always
—D. R.

In memory of Annie,
the blind opossum who
visited schools
—J. R.

A forest of poems

EAU DE FOREST:
A WOODSY COLOGNE

It's spiderwebs
and dogwood trees,
a muddy trail,
a blue-green breeze.

A nest, a leaf,
a sycamore trunk.
A whiff of pine,
a *hint* of skunk.

SPRING WELCOME

A million arms in woody sleeves
wave a zillion brand-new leaves,
inviting wrens to be their guests,
the orioles to build their nests,
and calling all the chickadees
to stay and raise their families.

BIOGRAPHY OF A BEAVER

Bucktoothed Cleaver
Tree Retriever
Building Conceiver
True Believer
Waterproof Weaver
Overachiever
Roll-Up-Her-Sleever—
Hooray for the Beaver!

THE GREAT SNAIL RACE
An Eyewitness Account

You should have seen the winning snail—
his handsome head, his silky tail,
the ripples in his gleaming hide,
his saddle rocking side to side.

You should have seen his pride and nerve,
the way he took the final curve.
He won the race in record time,
and what a *perfect* trail of slime!

WOODPECKER FEUD

A couple of woodpeckers bicker and tease,
pecking away at their separate trees.

One of them taps out a cutting remark
that shoots out a shower of sparks from the bark.

The other comes back with a heated reply
that sends up a tower of smoke to the sky.

They hammer and pound at a furious pace,
both of them rumpled and red in the face.

The argument ends with some hotheaded shrieks,
then neither one speaks to the other for weeks.

ODE TO A SALAMANDER

Ponder yonder salamander,
innocent and shy:
a sensitive amphibian
who wouldn't hurt a fly . . .
especially if there should be
a *spider* passing by,
which she could sweetly gobble up
and barely blink an eye.

DEAR BADGER, BELOVED—

Of all the fine badgers that I've ever known,
it's *you* that I'm longing to have for my own!
I swoon at the sight of your glorious face,
and no other badger could ever replace
your stinky perfume or that breathtaking snout,
the wobbly way that you waddle about.

One touch of your claws and I'm weak at the knees.
I'm asking sincerely—I'm begging you, please,
to give me a snarl or a threatening hiss.
Just send me a sign and I'll promise you this:
a badger who worships you—one who *adores*!
A badger who's truly and faithfully—

Yours

OPOSSUM'S MARSUPIAL DAYDREAM

Opossum dreams of kangaroos,
of wallabies and bandicoots—
the cousins she has never known.
She rambles through the woods, alone,
imagining their carefree days
somewhere *wild* and far away.

A WILD TURKEY COMMENTS ON HIS PORTRAIT

I find it most insulting
that you traced around your hand
and colored all my feathers
either plain old brown or tan.

Where's the copper? Where's the gold
that a turkey should expect?
Where on earth is raw sienna,
and where is the respect?

Finally, I'm baffled
that you've made me look so dumb.
My head is quite distinguished
and it's *nothing* like your thumb.

MOONLIT RACCOON

In a watery mirror
the rugged raccoon
admires his face
by the light of the moon:
the mysterious mask,
the whiskers beneath,
the sliver of cricket
still stuck in his teeth.

PROPOSAL FOR A SQUIRREL SPA

The squirrel's life is run, run, run—
it seems her work is never done.
Those flying leaps, those frantic trots.
Those teeny shoulders tied in knots.

So I propose a squirrel spa—
someplace very la-di-dah,
with all the walnuts she can eat
and pedicures for all four feet.

She'll have the time to ease her mind,
to let her curly tail unwind.
A week of lounging in the grass
and possibly a yoga class.

TURTLE BEACH

I'm just a simple turtle,
and this is all I ask:
a shallow stream for swimming,
a quiet place to bask . . .

plus . . . a ray or two of sunshine
on my humble strip of sand . . .
and . . . a boulder for my pillow
would be absolutely grand.

Then . . . a sturdy log for floating,
an energizing snack,
a bird to entertain me,
and some lotion for my back.

Oh, sure . . . I'd love a towel
or a sip of lemonade.
But I'm a simple turtle.
That's *not* the way I'm made.

HOW TO RECOGNIZE
A GREEN TIGER BEETLE

When you're walking through the woods
with a beetle at your heel—
a high-gloss beetle
who's a brilliant shade of teal—
and she twinkles in the sun
like a beetle made of steel,
that's a Green Tiger Beetle,
and she's absolutely real.

TOAD'S LUNCH

The juicy mosquito
I snagged in midair
was uncommonly good,
yet it didn't compare
to the tongueful of ants
that I licked off the dirt,
which would melt in your mouth
like the sweetest dessert.
But I made a mistake
with the slug-on-a-stick—
a *smidgen* too salty—
and now I feel sick.

A TREE FROG'S LAZY AFTERNOON

Her tree house has an open door
and she can hear the raindrops pour
along the roof and down the eaves
on shingles made of soggy leaves.

Here, inside her cozy bunk,
tucked in tight against the trunk,
she glances at the gloomy skies
and pulls the shades across her eyes.

NOBODY'S PET
A Word to the Wise from a Red Fox

I will *never* take walks
in the park wearing socks
like some spoiled little dog
on a leash—I'm a *fox*.

I won't come when you call,
I won't jump for the ball,
I won't wait for your step
like a lump in the hall.

You can tell me to *stay*
if you want to, but hey—
there's no way in the world
that I'll ever obey.

OCTOBER SURPRISE PARTY

Above my head a robin sings
a shy *hello* and flaps her wings.
She whistles to a waiting squirrel,
who gives his fuzzy tail a twirl
and bounces on a flimsy branch,
which starts a leafy avalanche
of red and gold from every tree,
as if they've planned it all for me.

CHIPMUNKS, INC.

They work all day
in pinstriped suits
without a word of thanks,
faithfully investing
in the Acorn Savings Banks.

THE FOREST'S ROYAL FAMILY

In golden coats and velvet crowns
the deer inspect their royal grounds—
their breezy castles rising high,
their kingdom built of trees and sky.

THE NIGHT OWL

Somewhere in the forest
he is practicing his hoot,
but you'd swear that he's rehearsing
on a spooky-sounding flute—
working on his timing
and his quavery technique,
patiently perfecting
the position of his beak.

COYOTE CAROLERS*

Coyotes in the falling snow
are singing all the songs they know—
the good old-fashioned favorites
and all the big coyote hits.

Bundled up in furry coats,
belting out their highest notes,
they lope across the winter woods
to serenade the neighborhoods.

They sing until their throats are sore—
all night long their voices pour
coyote music through the air.
If no one listens,
they don't care.

*"Coyote" is pronounced
   as *ky-OH-tee*.

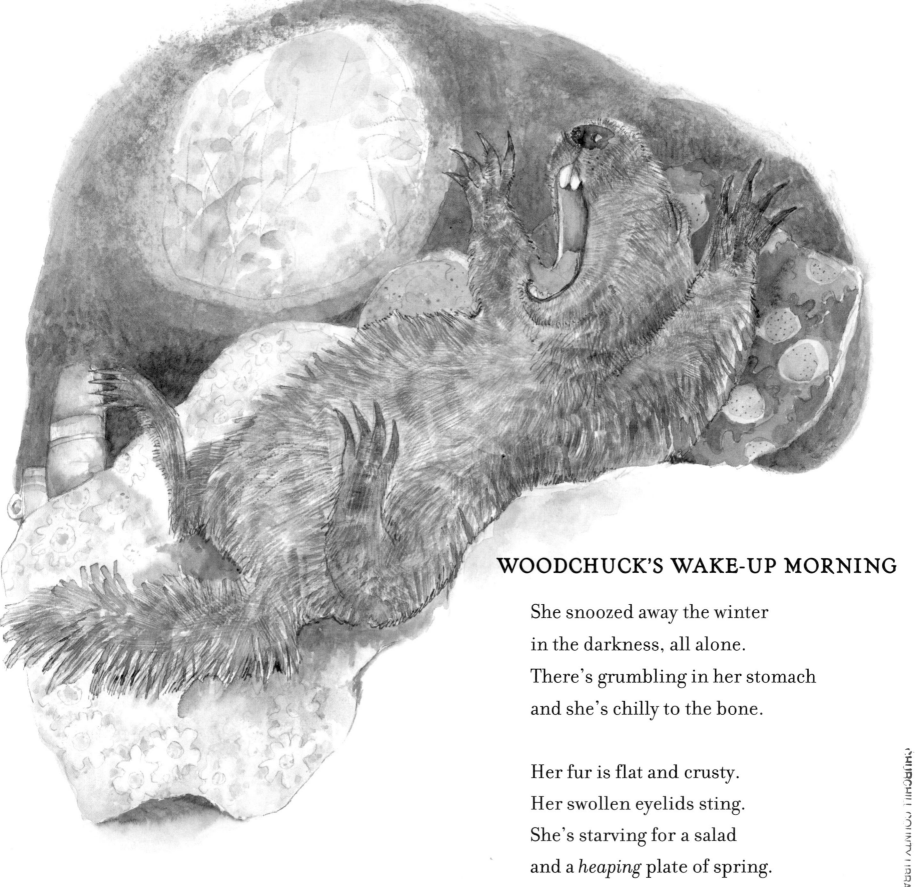

WOODCHUCK'S WAKE-UP MORNING

She snoozed away the winter
in the darkness, all alone.
There's grumbling in her stomach
and she's chilly to the bone.

Her fur is flat and crusty.
Her swollen eyelids sting.
She's starving for a salad
and a *heaping* plate of spring.